Shanty Coal City

Shanty Coal City

Novella

Gift Foraine Amukoyo

Soft Grid Limited

Gift Foraine Amukoyo

Published by

Soft Grid Limited

Plot 6, Block 23, Satellite Town

Calabar, Cross River, Nigeria

+234 (0)8027676550, +234 (0)8053110637

E-mail: softgridbooks@gmail.com

softgridltd@hotmail.com

www.softgridbookslimited.com

© Gift Foraine Amukoyo

First Published in 2018

ISBN 978-978-56095-2-3

Soft Grid Books

First Printing, December 2018

For a restructured and better society

CHAPTER ONE

Inferknow was tattily organized. The crudely built low-cost houses were in robust quantities and never short of occupants. Thin walls that separated a tenant from the other made it seemed, conversations from individual apartments emanated from one town hall meeting. In this crippling society, no act stayed private. Residents consciously watched out for all sorts of danger, from flying bottles to stray bullets.

Shacks lined by the shore were most expensive. People who lived close to the lakeside were privy to feed fishes with their waste and suck in bits of fresh air. Passersby covered their noses due galling stench that oozed of decaying human faeces. The neighbourhood needed health environmentalist intervention before a conceivable disease outbreak would befell every inhabitant.

Near the open canal, some teenage boys played card game on a worn out snooker board. A fight broke out over cheaters and the shaken snooker board turned into a wrestling ring. Girls took turn in skipping and danced in the fast swinging tiny ropes. A six-year-old boy, cried with half bucket of cold buns on his head.

The boy recalled his mother warning him. *'Don't return with a single bun or else, you would have your tongue for dinner. Do I make myself clear?' He nodded.*

He was lucky. Some gangsters asked the reason for his distress. The gangsters bought the entire snack and distributed to the children around. A woman, smoking cigar by a water tank patted his back and gave him Two Hundred Naira. He rolled the money into tiny fold then hid it in his bushy hair and gave her a soldierly salute.

The town was a rustling ground for witty man, woman and children with sinew limbs. Laziness only fetched hunger, starvation, denigration and oppression; beggars did not strive on these streets.

The population was multifaceted. Assigned census officials always had difficulty keeping head count of the people who lived in Inferknow. Residents did not abide by moral of the society but to dictates of hard street life, a harsh fate of trying realities. The imposing downtrodden system did not threaten these people. Their worry was how to manage the world's circumstances as best as they could. They held belief that a great instrument of change could be born amongst one of them; they just needed a reason to keep up with the struggle, and maybe a light would shine at the end of this dark tunnel.

CHAPTER TWO

It was in the evening that most night traders arrange their wares in makeshift stalls. It was not the usual petty provision stores found on most rugged streets. This was the suburb of Inferknow lit with beautiful street spotlights, and the vendors' choices of goods rated eighteen.

A sassy young woman walked up to a kiosk. The trader slightly raised his head from the radio. He had bent low to catch football highlights from the screechy radio. He got up abruptly on seeing one of his regular customers. Her aura was irrepressible. When she walked down the street, people turned their heads and fixated eyes on her rosy attractive figure.

The trader came very close to her. As her secret admirer, he loved to sniff her scent whenever she came by. She leaned heavily on the door of the kiosk. "Hey Protocol, let me have one pack of condom and a small bottle of whiskey, quickly." She chewed gum and made round bubbles with the gum.

He looked dreamily at her visible cleavages, sexily accentuated by her low neckline gown, "is it for woman or man?"

She irritatingly snapped her fine polished nails in his face. "Are you blind, can you not see the buyer is a woman, or when have I ever bought a male condom from you?" She hissed.

Petrified she might pierce his eyes with her sharp pointed nail tips, he withdrew his face, "these days, I just confuse." He picked her order and handed the items to her in a transparent nylon.

"Please take your money and make sure to give me my complete change." She threw the money in his face.

He caught the One Thousand Naira note. He put the money in one side of his deep pockets. "Oh sissy, is there nothing for the boys?"

"Because you follow me work the work or what? Stingy goat like you, be suffocating your erectile penis behind your stupid kiosk. You should come into the brothel for some hot sexual pleasure, stingy fool."

He was shocked she knew his penis was erect, "oh sissy, you too much."

"Hmmm, one day, I will deal with your criminal ways. You think you are very smart, eh. See your face like used condom. All my small, small naira with you is enough to build a bungalow in my village."

The trader grinned at the fact that he was really making some fortune from his regular customers. He brought out money from the other pocket to pay the balance. After counting the money to be sure it was complete, the woman seductively walked through a black gate.

Women of diverse shapes, sizes and complexions moved around, scantily clad.

"Faith, was it condom you went to buy?" Mama asked.

"What else would have taken me out at this time of the day? I went to get some working tools. I have an emergency customer. He wants some hot shots for the cold weather," she smiled wantonly.

"Please, can I have some?"

"Mama, I am not even sure this would be enough for me. The way I'm seeing that guy, it seems he is sexually starved."

Mama laughed softly, "So he is really horny, eh. Okay, let me not delay you. I hope, Protocol, still has some condoms. The way business is booming, a condom firm needs to site its manufacturing company in Good Evening Street." They laughed.

Two girls conversed about Mama. They were at a lousy game of ludo that made their conversation inaudible to stray ears. "Just look at her, what an old shameless woman." Fassa said.

"When will she retire from the trade for young sweethearts like us to deal in?" Gwen said. She appraised her sexy figure and pushed up her breasts, already emphasized by her expensive padded bra.

Fassa admired her own glistening skin. "I wonder oh my sister. Out of all the customers that troop in here for pleasure, she gets almost thirty per cent of the men. She does that with ease while we have to struggle to get ten customers in a day."

"Please don't exaggerate. But I wonder what young and old men see in her old shrunken vagina."

"I think she uses juju to boost her hustle. I heard that she goes to a medicine man once in a while to renew her charms."

"I thought it was her daughter she goes to visit. She takes with her, foodstuffs for her daughter who is a nurse."

"And you believe that rubbish? Girl, you fall my hand. Those are just formats to disguise her movements. Does she really have a daughter? Have you ever seen a soul come to visit her as mother or a kin?"

"Babe, you are incredible. What child would be proud of her mother doing harlotry and want to be seen around her area of operation?"

"Is Grace's child not living with her?"

"Come on, that baby is still a toddler. Gwen, it is nothing comparable. Besides, Grace is an insane woman. What sort of mother will bring up a child in this kind of environment? A daughter for that matter, my prayer for that baby is that her mother retires from this trade before she becomes a teenager. That woman is not okay at all, she must be insane. She may even sell out her daughter in this trade from the slutty way she dresses that child." Fassa sighed at the possibility, and cleared her winning seeds from the ludo board.

"You think you are making too much sense with your talks and winning the game same time, right?"

"You sound as if you've ever beaten me at the game." Fassa threw the dices on the board, "if that woman has a child as claimed, then I give her kudos for given her daughter a good life. I can stake my games she used this prostitution work to train her daughter to wherever she is today."

"Hmmm, you're right. It is nice if that is really the case. Now that I think of it, that Grace is really a stupid woman. I pray we make enough money to start our photography and makeup business. We need to get away from this brothel so we can marry and have our children in a good neighbourhood. I really want to be a full time photographer," Gwen said.

"My dream is to do a makeover for brides and celebs. I pray God helps us to achieve our dreams." Fassa said. They chorused *Amen* and got serious on the game.

Here, prostitution was a daytime business. Wings of its regional association protected it. The women no longer hid their business. Only those without permit ran away when task force of the association come to raid for illegal practitioners. The byelaws protected rights of the sex workers from clients who refused to pay for their services or tried to harass them.

CHAPTER THREE

Some workers carried heavy equipment on their heads and shoulders. They sturdily and swirly walked on distorted staircase. A stout young man with well-defined and visible muscles lifted a rod off the sagging shoulder of an old man and carried it to one of the warehouses.

Borrows Steel Company was first in the city to run for more than two years. Sited in a densely populated area with cheap mass labour that toiled day and night, it was on a fast track to gain recognition as third largest in the colony. It ridiculed the living standard of local communities through its shady wage packages and unstable employment rate.

The facility was risk proven environment for it workers. On daily basis, workers prayed against danger as they worked without safety precautions. The workers heard heavy ticking sound from the central clock. It marked end of the day's job. After they cleaned up their sweaty bodies with dirty shirts, they lined up and filled their personal data on a piece of paper to receive their wages.

The Contractor came to applaud them for today's efforts with a repugnant remark they were, 'pacesetters other job seekers should emulate.' He scrutinized the names on the list and handed cash to the Supervisor to pay them. Satisfied with how the Supervisor doled out the envelopes, the Contractor entered a Range Rover car, parked outside rotted iron gates. The road was chock-full with sluggish workers. He bellowed for the driver to hoot the car's horn.

He brought out a handkerchief from his shirt pocket and wiped sweat off his forehead. "I can't miss my appointment. Please hoot the car's horn for these fools to get their lazy feet out of the way."

"Yes sir." The driver put on the stereo. He hummed as his favourite song came on air. He sang the lyrics, *'Oh baby cool o…cool o and shake your waist for me. My baby you hot o…you fine o…make you twist that thing for me. Oh, I will spend all my money on you.'* "Oga, I know you like this song too." He increased the radio's volume and smiled. He bobbed to the song's beat.

"I don't like the song. Keep quiet and drive." He removed the helmet from his sweaty baldhead, "turn on the AC. I wonder how these people work in this heat. They must be adaptive to hell," he pulled off his heavy work boots, "and turn off the radio!"

Although the driver was accustomed to his boss's unpredictable mood swings, the outburst confused him because he had seen him dance to the song at clubs. The Contractor could pay any DJ on wheels to play the song nonstop.

The road did not have a good drainage system. The patched repairs on both sides were a pool that made the road badly congested. As the people gave way for the car to pass through, the driver moved slowly in order not to splash muddy water on them.

This was his first day at work. Ezekiel counted monies paid for the new daily job that would last for six months. He was disappointed. The wad of cash in the envelope turned out to be Two Thousand disbursed in Two Hundred Naira denomination. When he and others took on the job, they had no idea of the salary scale. The swell envelope handed to him and his colleague made them hopeful the pay would offset some pressing needs.

Ezekiel was stunned. There was no way he could save out of this peanut. He thought of quitting. The job agent he would pay ten per cent from his salary had told him this job involved good payment. He made a mental note of the amount of debt he had to pay before reaching home. He would have to go by the canal to dodge his creditors. Ezekiel scoffed and walked on.

CHAPTER FOUR

Few hours later, Chief Daggers smiled when the Contractor carried a big leather bag into his private sitting room. He unzipped it to reveal neatly arranged dollar notes. Chief Daggers rubbed his palms together and danced energetically to oppression of the poor workers.

"The Don himself, I told you it would work, this is your gateway to riches." Chief Daggers said.

"Yes Chief, I believe. Those people are dumb, especially the youths. They did not even ask what the form was. The workers just signed to flattened stomachs." They barked sinister laughter.

"I told you, that is how it works in the ministry, if a few bark, just call them to a corner and settle them with bonuses, and watch how they get busy, digging ground to save it for time to time licking and cracking."

"Yes, you said so. They will surely bark and tear at each other's throats like hypnotised bulldogs."

The maid served them drinks. They clank glasses of wine unaware of her repulsive stare. She loathed their remarks. She did well to hide her disdain from the bosses. "Distasteful people, oh, I wish I had spat in those glasses of wine," she mumbled.

"Elizabeth, why are you still here? Do you want to be relieved from your duties?" Chief Daggers asked.

"No sir, no sir, I beg your pardon," said Elizabeth. She clasped the empty gold tray to her chest and scurried off to the kitchen.

The men proceeded to an exclusive study in deep conversation. Once in, the Contractor flopped onto an armless chair and stretched his legs.

"Now, you would have to fill another form. Instead of the Two Thousand Naira paid to them, you would put in the bespoke Ten Thousand Naira contracted by the Government. Compile the list, and transfer the Minister of Labour' share of the money to his account," said Chief Daggers.

"Well done, Chief Daggers." The Contractor said. "The way you inflated the project by Five Hundred Million Naira really amazed me. I thought the little additional millions you had spoken about was something mild, you're indeed a smart man." He sipped wine.

"My brother, that is how we built this luxurious lifestyle and we must maintain it at any cost." They laughed and clinked glasses.

Jerry came in without knocking. "Dad, guess what, my friend, Dan, is having his birthday party in America and I will need to use your private jet."

"Sure son, and have fun at the party. My boys will put some things in place," Jerry looked confuse. Chief Daggers quickly said, "They will put things in place for your comfort."

"Oh, okay dad, you're the best. Thank you." He did a thumb up at his father.

"You're welcome, son. I hope you had a nice time at the race course today?"

"Sure I did. We tested our wheels on the major roads. However, there was just a little accident. My bike crushed a pregnant woman. She did not survive. We were lucky your police friend rescued us from an angry mob."

"That's my boy. Feisty, fast and furious. Son, come say hello to my friend. Forget about the incidence. It was the woman's time to go. Later, I shall speak to the Inspector."

Jerry shook hands with the Contractor. "I'm pleased to make your acquaintance. I am Jerry Daggers, the humble business tycoon's son."

"You don't need an introduction. The resemblance is striking. It tells me your father was indeed a very handsome man in his youth. Be glad you're born into a great dynasty."

"It is the Lord's doing, my brother." Chief Daggers proudly said while Jerry threw his bike keys and caught the keys mid-air as he made his way out.

Ezekiel dropped the envelope that contained painkiller on the bed. He sat on the single chair in the room. His house was so neat and well arranged for a one room in a shanty. He could not relax without a bath. He scratched his chin and abdomen.

He perceived his armpit and made a funny face at the unpleasant smell. He went to the bathroom. An empty drum he had filled to the brim greeted him. Ezekiel had filled the drum with water in the morning and secured it with a strong padlock before he left for work.

"Oh no, not again," he rubbed his full hair in frustration. It was not as if he fancied afro hairstyle, his hair had missed the barber's clipper for so many weeks because he was conscious of not spending his earning spectacularly. This was his first job after his retrenchment from an insurance company.

Angrily, Ezekiel thought why some of his neighbours had to finish the whole water, and not take some pails as they did on many occasions. He was tired of most of his neighbours fetching out of his drum as if it was the compound's reservoir. "Ah. I wish I could give them thorough wash in the sea and drown them." He clawed his fingers and bared his fangs.

Unlike most tenants in the compound that had younger siblings or children they could send to fetch water at regular intervals, Ezekiel did not have that kind of luxury. Therefore, he usually filled his drum before going to hustle every morning. He quickly had his bath with a bag of sachet water and cleaned the soapy part of his body with a face towel. He had few minutes to meet up his friend for an evening hangout.

Two women sat at a round working table. It was the nursing department of Peace Corps. They were working late into the night. The office was quiet as they were busy writing the week's report on their field works.

The Director had given them a three hour deadline, which they had thirty minutes more to round up. Gloria was a military nurse while Rachel was a civilian nurse. Gloria stood to get cold water from the dispenser.

"Make that two please." Rachel called out.

"One for me too please, I need warm water. The sour throat is killing me," Temba, the secretary kindly said.

"I've told you to put off the AC if it bothers you that much," Gloria said.

"And I said not to worry, girls. Ladies, I don't want to discomfort you guys for my own convenience." Temba coughed softly.

"Leave the babe; she probably wants to enjoy better coolness here. They might be power outage when she gets to her house." Rachel said and giggled.

"Rachel, be serious for once in your life." Temba said and threw a balled paper at Rachel.

"You are really not serious about getting well." Gloria put off the AC on her way back to sit and drew the blinds up.

Temba smiled. "Thank you, now I feel better."

"I know you would. You are welcome."

Rachel enthusiastically punched a key on the keyboard. "Wow! Thank God, it's Friday, who else is up. I'm so done with this report." Rachel waved three movie tickets she took out of her bag. "Who is interested?" She fanned her face with the tickets and patted her hair.

"Three movie tickets, babe you have money oh," Gloria said.

"For where, who has money to spare on these things, me? A beau gave the tickets to me. He knows we are the three musketeers in town. So you ladies have two, I can't leave you girls out of this fun." She wriggled her waist on the seat.

"Which of the beaus?" Gloria asked.

"Tell us." Temba urged her.

"The one at the mall." Rachel grinned.

"Girl, please don't take advantage of that guy. I can really see love in his eyes. He's got hot love for you babe." Gloria warned.

"Really, if you feel that much pity for him, then you can go ahead and reciprocate his affection. Not me babes, I am a free thinker. I am just catching my fun with no strings attached. It is not my fault he feels otherwise."

"Hmmm, Rachel, don't say I didn't warn you." She looked to Temba. "My sister, you're my witness, I hope I've said the right thing?" Temba nodded and Rachel stuck out her tongue at them.

The intercom buzzed and Gloria got it for Temba who was coughing a bit violently. "Hello sir, it's Gloria on the line."

"Gloria, send Rachel to my office immediately."

"Okay, sir," Gloria hung up and swung her chair to face Rachel. "Rachel, the Director wants you in his office."

Rachel hissed and adjusted her wig, "I wonder what he wants. I've just sent my report to his email."

"Why don't you go and see for yourself instead of mumbling useless hymns in our ears." Gloria said.

Rachel played with her computer keyboard, "I am fagged out. I don't have the strength to walk down the stairs."

"There is an elevator in this building. No delay, babe." Gloria said.

"Move your lazy ass." Temba said. She coughed.

Rachel stood and shook her buttocks in front of Temba, "not too lazy to give some sound tweaks."

"Rachel, the Director wants you in his office. Quit fooling around and get going before I smack your bums with the intercom." Gloria said.

"Yeah, I'm going, I'm going," Rachel played with Gloria's hair and turned on the AC. She quickly walked out before Gloria's condemnatory stare smothered her.

Rachel ran in front of the mall's entrance with enthusiasm of a schoolchild. Gloria and Temba came up to her.

"Rachel, you were to pay the cab man. But you didn't wait around to fulfil that, so dinner will be on you at home," Gloria said.

Rachel raised an eyebrow. "For what, please take back your money for the fare." She counted some money and gave to Gloria. "Dinner is more expensive. I would not be home anyway, remember I've a date tonight."

Gloria laughed, "Look at her, naughty girl. I thought you are a loaded babe. Next time, keep to the end of your bargain." The three women laughed and fell over one another as they made their way to the movie section.

Gloria tugged at Rachel's arm. "Rachel, Mike is waving at us. Come, let's go say hello to him."

"Please girls, we can do that later. Let's go and settle down for our movie; we don't want to miss the grand seats, do we?"

"I thought he gave you these movie tickets for free? You are unbelievable. Keep seats for us, we will join you." Gloria said.

Gloria and Temba walked towards the ticketing booth. Rachel hit her forehead with her palm and followed them to say hello to the grinning Mike. They quickly thanked him for the movie tickets and promised to call back after the show.

Mike was off duty and waited for the women. He smiled shyly on sighting Rachel. Gloria and Temba distant themselves, Rachel gave him a cold smile and walked pass him.

He pursued her, "hi, Rachel. Do you mind a glass of wine? There is a concert tonight at the Raven's Night Club. It is on the fourth floor."

Rachel stopped, "of course I know the club. I am not interested. I have a date tonight."

"Oh, okay. What about lunch tomorrow?"

"Mike, I am not really interested in going out with you. Thanks for the movie tickets. I really enjoyed myself. Bye." She walked away.

"Good night," Mike stared hard at her swinging hips and gave a curt salute to the swaying hips. He walked backwards and bumped into Gloria.

Gloria rubbed her shoulder, "whoosh I saw that coming."

"I am so sorry. I hope I did not hurt you?"

"Not a scratch. Thanks for the movie, Mike." Gloria said.

"You made our day so enjoyable." Temba said.

"It was my pleasure. Goodnight ladies."

CHAPTER FIVE

In the alleviated grime of Inferknow, two magnificent structures stood out. On major nights, both doors were widely opened until dawn. There were night of casting out demonic spells and parade of expensive coffin of drinks.

On last Fridays of the month, there was a sacrifice of virgins in the hotel. In an exclusive room, dogs on a bridal bed defiled underage girls for its patrons viewing pleasure. In the church, some ushers tied up possessed brethren to pillars to have them flogged by the pastor with confessional brooms and Holy Water.

The hotel was beside the religious house of worship. The church bell echoed for evening worship. Some patrons of the hotel felt uncomfortable whenever this bell clanged in the midst of their groans and moans. Inferknow was very lucrative for its business; the hotel management did everything possible for the church to move to another location. The hotel proprietor had secretly paid a surveyor to span the size of the church's land. Half of it encroached into the road and he anonymously wrote to the government.

Reputable for its jazz concept with lit Friday live band, it was one of its kinds in the colony, accessible and affordable with taste. Its norm of discretion also attracted many potential customers from everywhere.

It was very dim in the hotel's bar and restaurant. Joel clamped Ezekiel on his back. "Hey man! I see you're already down on the bottles."

"And the bill is on you. Why are you just getting here? I've been waiting for the past two hours and for that I think you owe me a coffin." They shook hands.

"You must be kidding me," Joel gave a throaty laugh.

"I have starched my buttocks on this stool for hours. I didn't call your phone because I took into consideration, whatever that had you preoccupied was very crucial."

"You're not far from the truth, Ezekiel. You nailed it perfect." Joel signaled for the bar tender to serve him a drink.

"Yeah, so what was the deal you had to keep me waiting so long?"

"Nothing much bro, I was held up in a traffic jam, it is crazy out there in the city. I wish my car could grow wings and fly off the frustrated roads."

"That's an expensive wish. My empty bank account excuses me from these luxurious complaints. I just alight from any bus and trek the rest way home or to any destination. These days, I don't find myself in a hurry."

"That's not funny, Ezy. We need to do something about your status. These suffer head pair of shoe on you embarrasses me, seriously." Joel chuckled.

"Have I ever refused new pairs from you? With your first grade okrika shirt-fairly used clothe, you could not even wash off the foul perfume. Look at this money-man that's so stingy to spend on his wardrobe." They laughed and Ezekiel gave Joel a light punch on his upper arm.

Joel collected his drink and took sips of the Irish cream. "Why did you prefer we hung out here?"

"The truth was I did not have enough money to transport myself uptown. It was embarrassing to blurt it on the phone."

"Easy man, it's Joel. We are like brothers." Joel prodded Ezekiel on his elbow.

"I know, Joel. But sometimes…"

"Sometimes, you need to put your pride aside. Do not let ego get in the way of our friendship, please. I think I know the Manager of Borrows Steel. We have had one or two business deals in the past. I would speak to him. Perhaps, you can work in a more refined section of that company."

"I would be glad. The pay will be better I hope."

"Certainly, you're a friend to the Manager's friend." Joel grinned.

Ezekiel laughed, "is that a company's rule?"

From behind them, they heard a familiar woman's sensuous voice. "Good evening handsome. Welcome to Good Evening Street Hotel and Brothel of fine wine. Do you want half a crystal glass of me or in full?"

"A half package is demeaning of silverware like you. I will take you full." The man appraised Faith from head to toe. Her good looks were stunningly sellable. She was seductively attractive with her voluptuous breasts and narrow waist; her buttocks will make any man's head, turn.

They bargained a price, fair to both, and Faith licentiously showed him the way to her room. Faith winked at Mama and Angela as she saw two clients approached them.

Faith walked pass Joel and Ezekiel with the man groping her buttocks. Neither of them uttered a word. Ezekiel patted Joel's crestfallen shoulder. Joel did not turn to see where they headed; his eyes drowned in anger and at the same time, love, that he found Faith after months of their separation. He put an ice cube in his mouth and crushed the cold slowly. Ezekiel took the glass cup from him and sipped the Irish cream.

With a large tip off, Joel got the room number of Faith from the waiter. An hour later, he rapped knocks on the door, before he could press the fourth; a familiar fragrance opened to him. He stepped into the room, uninvited and perceived yet, a distinct flavour that belonged to a rose and rotted thorns.

"What are you doing here?" Faith angrily demanded.

"Is that how to greet your love?" Joel's tone was icy.

"Don't play words with me. Say whatever brought you here."

"Faith, will you mince words with me?"

"I don't want you here."

"Where then will you have me?"

"Nowhere, please get out." She pointed him to the door.

Jaded by her rejections, Joel walked further into the room. Greatly offended by the mixed smell in the room, he tried to remain calm. "Do you miss my smell? Don't you toss around on your bed, missing me at night?"

"I do not."

"Did you miss my touch?"

"I've come to loath it. Do not mention your lips. I loathe every single kiss mine ever locked with it."

Joel spread his arms and turned around in the room. "So this is much preferable to my bed." He reached for her cheeks.

"Don't touch me, Joel, don't you dare take one step closer to me or else I'll scream and the bouncers will be here."

"Aren't they used to your screams? Your men must love it. I guess your screams make them increase your fees, right?"

"Stop it, Joel." She covered her ears with her hands.

"You can scream it will make no difference. Some horse dicks must be amongst your clients. They make you scream crazy, yeah?"

"I said stop it, stop it, Joel," she gave him a thunderous slap. He tasted blood in his mouth and he flexed his jaw.

"Stop it Faith, I just want to take you out of this hotel and to a better life, the way things used to be between us. No, not the way it was. It would be better, I promise."

"No, things can never be the same. This is how best the world can get for me. I'm queen of this kingdom, they call me goddess F because I make men shiver at the sight of my naked flesh and I can make them confess anything in the heats of orgasm."

"Confession of lies and lust, that's no life. Please baby, just give me a chance to make things right."

"It's too late. Go away from here, and don't ever show yourself to me."

Joel looked around the room covered with pink wall paint, purple embroideries and furniture. He cursed his mother for destroying his marriage. As soon as he shut the door, Faith allowed tears to troll down her cheeks.

In the adjacent room from Faith's, Angela was in a dilemma. Women who seldom traded sex booked part time rooms. Angela was unlucky on her fifth night. As usual, she had lain on the bed with her bra and chemise. Tonight, this man asked her to take off the rest of her clothes.

"I would have you completely naked."

"No sir, you paid for my vagina and not my whole body."

"What is this? Hey woman, listen here, I cannot have sex with a woman without fondling and sucking breasts. It is the greatest way for my little man to get into tough action."

"Sorry, I can't take them off."

"Then, there can't be business between us." He got up.

She stopped him from fastening his belt and looked up to him with pleading eyes. "Can't you just do it without my breasts?"

"You see my erection; it will triple in width and length as soon as it sees boobs. I need to get value for my money. I can see you have great watermelons on your chest. Let me have those juicy cups."

She finally gave in and began to remove the rest of her clothes. His penis went limp when she hesitatingly relieved her breasts from the tight cups. Her breasts almost reached her abdomen, and nipples dripped of milk.

"My God, what are you doing here? There is no way I am doing it with you; your baby must be crying so loud at home. Where is the father of the child? Why are you doing this?" He shockingly asked.

"He must be lying somewhere drunk in a gutter. Please. I really need this money. My baby is not at home, but in intensive care unit."

"I have a strong appetite for sex, but I can't be this extreme; I cannot do this with you. You should know better. Being soft spoken and your modest dress sense made me choose you in the first place. Get dressed, and then go back to the hospital to nurse your sick baby. Woman, try to trade in something more decent."

The man gave her Five Thousand Naira. Before he left, he gave her the address to his private hospital for her to bring her child for treatment.

Fassa and Gwen were curious on why he came out with a disgruntled look. He chose another woman. Her transparent gown highlighted her pointed nipples. From the grapevine, they later found out the client's encounter with Angela.

In order for their reputation to remain standing, the management decreed no flaccid breast should be among workers of Good Evening Street Brothel. Those who could afford it underwent breast surgeries and procured other enlargement enhancers.

CHAPTER SIX

Joel came out of a drug store. He was sad over how Faith had devalued her self-worth. As he pondered on ways to get her out of the life of squalor, someone bumped into him.

"Oh, I'm sorry."

"Oh, gosh, can't you see, lady?"

"Yeah, I'm so sorry." Tears gathered in her eyes.

Joel was touched and angry at his insensitivity. A person with correct eyesight would not have collided with another the way she had done.

"It is I who is sorry. I am sorry please. I did not have an idea. I should have taken care."

"No, I should have taken care." She tightly held to her cane.

"Don't make me feel guiltier. The fault is entirely mine. I guess you are going into the pharmacy. Getting some drugs I presume?"

"Yeah, I am."

"You should have asked someone to help you out instead of taking the risk of walking all by yourself."

"You're right but I don't have any help at my disposal for now."

"What about your parents, sibling, or any relation, where are they?"

"Please..." She was pained.

"I'm sorry, please pardon me if I've steered you in the wrong lane."

"Never mind, it's okay."

"So, we can get the drugs. You know the name of your medication, right?"

"Sure I do, sir. However, you need not worry; I do not want to delay you any further. I would be fine by myself."

"Well pretty lady, do me this honour."

"Oh, no, please."

"I insist, so it is either you lead the way, or I take the lead. Whichever way, I'm at your service."

She blushed. "Okay, thank you."

Joel carefully guided her into the store. He was amazed at every unaltered step she took.

"Hello Lillian, I hope you're feeling much better today." The pharmacy attendant asked.

"I'm fine, madam. Thank you."

"I see the two of you are well acquainted." Joel smiled at the attendant.

"Yes, she is one of our regular customers."

"Very well then, can you give me a pack of her drug?"

"No please, I just want half a sachet."

"Dear lady, how many is in a sachet?" He asked the attendant.

"It is six tablets, sir."

"What's her dosage?"

"Two tablets to be taken three times daily."

"Okay. I'm buying a pack."

"No please." Lillian reached for his arm and Joel held her to his side.

"Oh lady, please make it five packs."

Lillian was squirmy. "Stop sir, you don't know the cost. It's expensive."

"How much is it?"

"A pack is Five Thousand, Six Hundred Naira." The attendant answered; with hope, he was going to buy that much.

"That's quite expensive. I hope you have a POS here?" Joel asked.

"Sure sir, we have several." She smiled courteously and brought out three POS machines from below the counter.

"Great, let's have the drugs."

Lillian was stunned at the stranger's generosity. "Hey hold on, sir. I do not have money for payback. Please don't put me in such debt."

"It's a selfless service. Lillian, please let me do this, thanks."

"Thanks, I'm grateful. You know my name. I don't recall telling you."

"The lady attendant said your name on our arrival."

"Okay, that explains it. I almost took you to be a wizard." Joel laughed. They started a conversation while the attendant packaged the drugs.

True to Joel's words, Ezekiel got an available position in store keeping, but the risk was still present. He was fast to move his leg before a heavy bolt fell on him. His safety boot would not have saved him from getting hurt. He bent down to examine his foot.

Someone strolled to his side, "You were lucky."

Ezekiel looked up to the strange face. "You can say that again, but it slightly got my big toe. I am a bit hurt."

"You have to be more careful. This company has made many ex-workers cripple. The saddest thing is that, there is no compensation. The management leaves you to your pains."

Ezekiel nodded, "I know that much. This is my first time of seeing you here."

"I am Charles. I just got back from my one week leave."

"Welcome back. Pleased to meet you. I am Ezekiel, I am new here."

"Congratulations. You must be a diligent staff. You were here before eight o'clock. Do not show much eagerness. The Boss would overwork you until you are bone tired." He went to his locker to hang his shirt. Both of them began to work. They cleaned and greased bolts.

Later, they heard screaming from outside. Charles rushed out while Ezekiel limped forward and was on time to see someone falling down from a building. They reached downstairs, a crowd had gathered. When the workers dispersed, Ezekiel saw iron protruded the fallen man's heart. He held himself from throwing up. He spat on the ground and went upstairs.

Ezekiel knew he had to get a job elsewhere. When he got home, he updated his CV on his phone.

"Ezekiel," Bullock, his next-door neighbour called out. "Ezekiel, please come out. It is you that can solve this issue for us." Bullock wrapped an insistent knock with a stone on Ezekiel's door.

"Bullock, good evening," Ezekiel stretched his body and yawned. He posed at the entrance.

"Good evening, my brother. How was work?"

"Work was fine. What is the matter that you would not allow your neighbour rest after a hard day's job?"

"No vex. It's my woman's matter, is it…?"

"Bullock, you better come into this house and answer me." His girlfriend marched out of the house with wrapper loosely tied to her waist.

"Good evening, madam." Ezekiel said.

"Brother Ezekiel, good evening," she smiled and advanced on Bullock.

"She is here. Ezekiel, please judge this matter. Can a man not have peace because he is yet to pay his woman's bride price? Is it a crime I don't have the means yet?"

"You don't have the means to pay my bride price, but you had money to pay hospital bills when I had our baby? Now you want me to spread my legs again so that you can score another cheap goal, right?"

"You see, I have not said ten words, and she has spoken hundred words. Ezekiel, is this the kind of woman I will spend the rest of my life with? Have I said I will not marry you?"

She clapped her hands, "Your action says you will not marry me. You always avoid marriage discussions and you are ever ready to get between my thighs."

"My priceless jewel, please, let me have peace while I make enough money. I will come to see your people. Let me have peace."

"There is no peace for the wicked. Bullock, you are a wicked man. Pay my bride price or else there would not be peace in this house. How much is the dowry that you cannot honour me? Even after having your child?" Bullock spread his hands in wonder. His girlfriend jerked his wrapper and dragged him towards the house.

"Ezekiel, are you seeing this woman? Will you not talk to her?" His girlfriend dragged him to the doorstep and shoved him into their room.

Ezekiel groaned and went into his house. He applied balm on his legs. "Oh, I am yet to have my bath." He stood instantly and winced. He pulled off his clothes and tied a towel to the bathroom. He had his bath, dressed up and hurried to work.

Two days later, Ezekiel hurried to grease some bolts. After his morning shift, he went outside. At the foot of the staircase, he was busy refreshing his internet browser when Charles tapped his shoulder.

"Ezekiel, you are here."

"Yes, Charles."

"The Boss wants to see you in his office." Ezekiel put his phone in his pocket and dragged his feet to the office.

"Good morning, sir."

"It is surely a good morning for me. Let's find out what it is for you, young man." The soft-spoken Manager peered at him through his askew-medicated glasses. Ezekiel swallowed his warm saliva at the chilly tone.

"What kept you away from work for two days?"

"I'm sorry, sir. It was because I had…"

"You had what? What was so important that you had to abandon all your duties, you took leave off work without permission from your supervisor?"

"I'm very sorry, sir, truly I'm. I know there is nothing I can say that would placate my act. But please have mercy on me."

"What kept you away, Ezekiel?"

"I had an important errand to run, sir."

"Oh, I see, so you have a job more important than your work here?"

The inference of losing his job made him go down on his knees and put clasped hands on the Manager's desk. "No sir, please I'm truly sorry sir, I beg your pardon."

"Oh, get up, I don't like such, I am not one of those mediocre bullies. I will let this slid because the company has had no complain from you before, and you're one of our best recruits at the warehouse."

"Thank you, sir."

"But don't ever think you're indispensable."

"I know sir."

"You can go back to your duty post."

"Thank you, sir." Ezekiel bobbed and left the Manager's office.

Few minutes later, Ezekiel came into the Manager's office. He fidgeted as he coughed to get the engrossed man's attention from his laptop.

"Excuse me, sir."

"Yes Ezekiel, what is it?"

"It is an urgent matter?"

"Then speak. What has come over you lately, are you sure you are all right?"

"It is about some personal matters."

"Then tell me young man, you can see I've a lot of work on my desk."

"Sir, I just realized my phone is out of data subscription."

"Am I to buy data for you or this company should provide you with a free Wi-Fi?"

"No sir, I don't need a wife."

With a stupefied look, "you're not a dummy, Ezekiel. It is a Wi-Fi, not wife. They do not even sound common. Have you gone crazy? I think you are just out of your mind with worry. Say what you want before you irritate me with more stupidity."

"Sir, I need time off, just enough to get to the cyber café to check out my email box."

"Okay, you may have the day off and be the first person to resume at work tomorrow." Ezekiel profusely thanked him and ran off.

CHAPTER SEVEN

Ezekiel was on time for an interview. He composed himself and walked gently to take a seat. He was yet to relax when the Secretary announced his name. She directed him to a conference room. He greeted the panel of interviewers, and then sat for the instant written test and oral interview.

On his way home, Ezekiel hoped to get the job. He was sure he did well in the test and answered the interviewers' questions well enough. He hit his ankle on a big stone and let out a painful howl. He winced and jogged on one leg to a business centre-a local stand where vendor sell airtime vouchers.

Gloria was buying recharge card. She empathised with him and vacated the only seat under the umbrella. "Sit down. You have hurt your ankle badly. The cut is quite deep. You should go to a clinic. It's just around the corner, you can take a tricycle."

"I would have, but I don't have cash on me."

"Okay not to worry, just take a leap and help me carry you down to that official Hilux by the roadside. I will just take you to our clinic. I'm a nurse from the Peace Corps unit."

"Aren't I lucky? Thank you, please help me." Gloria assisted Ezekiel to the vehicle. She explained to the driver and he drove down to the clinic.

At the clinic, Gloria did the last stitches with coverings on his wound and sprayed an antidote to prevent itching and keep it dry. Ezekiel smiled as she removed the gloves to sanitise her hands.

"Thank you, you've saved me today."

"Don't mention. Just make sure to take your drugs and come back for change of plaster, and let's see how the foot is doing, okay?"

"Wouldn't it be wise I do a follow up treatment in a local pharmacy? I mean to cut cost. I don't even know how much bill I owe your clinic right now."

"Oh, no, it is free. I have registered your card with One Thousand Naira only. It is a NHIS scheme by the Government, so you can receive treatment in state owned medical centres. You just have to renew your membership card every month with half the price."

"Oh my, should I say it is a fortune I got hit today? I have never heard of this initiative before. I know of NHIS, but I never thought it is accessible to poor guys like me."

"It is for everybody. That is why we are in the city to sensitise people about NHIS. The underprivileged should be aware and take advantage of it."

"I will share the word in my neighbourhood. Get ready for your clinic to be flooded. Thanks a lot."

Gloria laughed. "No problem, may God grant all good health. The hospital is not a fun place to be. Here is something to get you home."

He was surprised at her giving him money. "No, I can't take that. I've stressed you more than enough."

"Take it as a loan. You can repay me when you come back to the clinic."

Ezekiel accepted the money. "Thank you," Gloria smiled a warm welcome.

She helped him out of the hospital and boarded him into a tricycle, popularly known as 'keke'. Ezekiel profusely thanked her as she yet, settled the fare. He wondered if there really was an angel guiding him. He looked forward to repaying all her good deeds.

CHAPTER EIGHT

Jerry and his three friends got an arrest at the American Airport. The DEA found cocaine worth $10 Million in two suitcases in Chief Daggers' private jet. They found it after a search; an anonymous informant had disclosed the details to the DEA. Jerry was unsuspicious of the drugs stashed in the plane.

"I am not a drug addict so what will I be doing with a truck load of it?" He hollered at the search party.

Some minutes later, an officer showed him two suitcases filled with drugs, "One of these was pierced, and a white powder exposed, which tested positive."

"What, how could this be?" Jerry was shocked.

"Your body system might be free, but these cases contain tape wrapped packages weighing approximately one kilo," another officer said.

The aircraft crew were questioned about the luggage before they were discharged but Jerry and his friends were handcuffed and charged for drug trafficking.

Three people held a meeting in the executive lounge of Prime Royal Hotel. They deliberated on the likely competitors that had given information to the DEA and put the youngsters in the clutches of death.

Carlos, the hard-hearted of them all cared not about the lives at stake; he was angered about millions of dollars lost, "If that cocaine had been cut and sold on the streets, it would have had a potential value in excess of $100 million. Damn, this loss is unimaginable," he doused his cigar on the ashtray and took a long ragged smoke from a new cigar. "Chief Daggers, I thought you have become bolder and have resourceful middlemen in this game. The failed attempt to get those drugs into the country has caused us a fortune."

"Is that all you care about, the dollars? My son, my poor son will be sentenced to death for nothing."

Carlos waved off Chief Daggers, "Oh, damn your son's fate. We will talk about the dollar bills. Money has brought us to the fold of greed. What has happened is not a new thing. Need I remind you, that my son was on that jet too? Or do we rather give up ourselves to the American authorities to save our children? Remember the oath of secrecy and allegiance to the godfathers. They do not know you when the holocaust breaks out. If I were you, I will just pray in advance, for the repose souls of our children. I did that the minute I got the unfortunate news. You are luckier that he is not your only child. Unlike me, I just lost the only child I have."

"Smart talks, Carlos. That is a good counsel you dished to Chief Daggers and I hope he heals with it. Now to the main discuss of our meeting. Since the authorities now suspect the shipment to be overseen from this colony, we have to device other channels, another modus operandi of smuggling these suitcases." Mrs Lawson said.

"We should go through water, we use the cargoes." Chief Daggers said absentmindedly.

"The maritime cargo routes are stale as the dragon's fire. Chief Daggers, do not let the emotions of your son's predicament override your senses, please. The securities have become stricter; the navy and customs checks are really a nuisance. In the US, we are the most important distributors of heroin, from importing it into the country to distribution level and selling it to lower-level street gangs, so we have to be extremely careful not to lose our formation. It is good, the tubers of yams arrived in America with no stress. The weed would have flooded the market. The jet's failed return is just our woe." Carlos said.

The party dispersed. Chief Daggers stayed behind and drank himself to stupor. He did not have the guts to face his bereaved wife and children at home. She had come to know of his miscellaneous dealings, but she kept calm when he reassured her of the business safety. She warned him not to come home without her son or else she would let the whole world know of his atrocities. His associates must not come to know his wife had knowledge of their underworld deals; her life would be at stake.

CHAPTER NINE

Ezekiel just finished dressing his bed when he heard a soft knock on the door. He paused to be sure it was his door. There were times he had answered the knocks of Bullock' visitors. The sound came again, and a female voice asked if anyone was home. He sprayed little of his cologne around the room, previewed the room setting and rushed to get the door. He slightly opened the door to see who it was.

"Hey hi Gloria," he opened the door wider. "I thought you would call me when about to hit the road. I would have come out to the bus stop to wait for you. I didn't know you would trace the house so easily."

"I just followed the text description you sent to me. The residents have rich knowledge of people living here. I just had to ask three persons and they pointed the way until I got here."

Ezekiel laughed. "Yeah, this is Inferknow, you'll actually think nobody knows you, but they are geniuses in chronicling one's biography. Please come in." Gloria entered and thanked him.

Gloria looked around the room in open admiration. "Wow, your apartment totally looks different from what it is on the outside. It is beautiful, I love your taste."

Ezekiel smiled shyly. "Thank you, this is my humble haven. I had this furniture from my previous lifestyle. Most couldn't fit in so I donated it to an orphanage."

"That is impressive. You could have sold it or something."

"Nah, I can always get better ones." Ezekiel said with conviction. He was hopeful that these hard times in his life would pass. He had not wanted Gloria to come visit in this neighbourhood, but she insisted. He was grateful she found his apartment tasteful. "Come on, please sit down."

Gloria sat on the beautiful love seat. There was a demarcation from the living room with double cream curtains. She had a peek of his charming bedroom. The insulated bedroom was good for one to have quality rest, enjoyment and intimacy. He cleared his throat. Gloria turned her attention on him. He indicated the bedroom with raised eyebrow. She flushed and looked at the floor.

Ezekiel brought out a pack of juice and a clean glass cup. "I am sorry I don't have food in the house."

"Oh, don't embarrass me Ezekiel, I didn't come to party. I came to see how my friend is doing."

He picked up his wallet from the portable home theatre speaker. "Notwithstanding, you should have something to eat. I will get fresh snacks from a nice store down the road."

"Please don't bother. I see your wound is healing nicely." She pointed at his leg.

"Yes, the medications are a life saver. Thank you so much."

Gloria nodded and sipped the drink Ezekiel poured for her. In the course of their conversation, it was time for him to take his drugs.

"It is time for you to have your drugs. Have you eaten?"

"No, I will take the pills and eat later," said Ezekiel.

Gloria stopped him from opening the pills, "please show me to your cooking area."

"Don't tell me you want to cook for me. Please, do not bother. I can manage that."

"Ezekiel," she said with a warning tone of a nurse to a stubborn patient about to get an injection.

Ezekiel could not talk her out of preparing food. He dutifully showed her to the back of the house that directly faced a lagoon. Birds of beautiful plumage inhabited it. Green leaves and dirt streamed on the lake.

A fisherman entered the canoe, and took paddles in his hands and slowly moved towards the centre of the stream. Its waves seemed to be rising, and at a distance, looked ready to swallow the sojourner, but when he entered the brackish edge, the waves calmed. However, no sooner was one garland of foam dissolved, than other more intimidating wave arose and its force capsized the canoe. The fisherman took a leisure swim.

Ezekiel aided her to cook concoction spaghetti with lots of onions and crayfish to spice. His drugs would induce him to sleep, so Gloria took her leave after they ate. Before the pills doused him to sleep, he thought it had been long he had someone fret over him. Ezekiel hugged a pillow and smiled at the luxury of such feeling.

CHAPTER TEN

In the night, Bullock called on Ezekiel. He told him he had perceived the aroma of his meal but he was busy inside with his girlfriend, if not, he would have come out for a portion.

He advised Ezekiel to marry Gloria because it was a 'quality wife material' that can 'arrange quick meal' where there was no money and the kitchen had scarce ingredients. He told Bullock, that Gloria was just a friend.

"How can a man be just a friend with a beautiful woman he spends hours with in a room, and she also goes through the stress of cooking for him?" Bullock asked bemused. Ezekiel did not try to explain the possibility to a man like Bullock.

Bullock shared some jokes and dating tips with Ezekiel, before he headed off to his business. He wheeled a truck of ten jerry cans and whistled a ghetto tune. Ezekiel shook his head at the man he suspected to be in shady businesses, yet no police had come looking for him, so he felt the jolly good fellow did an innocent risky business. Bullock had told him he did not mind if there was crude scarcity or not. He said he preferred going at night to buy diesel from tankers who wanted to boycott selling to fuel stations.

Bullock stopped humming when he reached the junction. He looked sideways, glanced backward and veered in the right direction. He stopped at the isolated location where the telecommunication tower was and untied a very long hose from underneath the truck.

Of recent, long queues formed at petrol stations across the colony had caused untold hardship for motorists and people who relied on generators to generate electricity. This had triggered increase in price of food commodities, transport fare and general cost of living.

The telecommunication company had threatened to shut down its operations across the colony due to diesel shortage. Bullock neither owned a phone nor sim card, which was why he cared less as he spanned the telecom tower and smirked at the goldmine he was about to strike.

The tower consumed about 1.4 Million litres of diesel to power base transceiver stations, and Bullock just needed two hundred litres. The co-located tower housed three to five base stations and the 27KVA generator had a refill this morning. Bullock got the news from the tank driver that offloaded the commodity.

When he was done with the extraction, Bullock brought out a fresh wrap of weed and lit it. As he smoked the leaves airily, he thought of how to give his girlfriend lots of money in a day or two. It would make her widely spread her fleshy thighs that drove him crazy. He chuckled and licked his lips in anticipation.

The smell of the weed attracted a police patrol van, and they traced the scent to the tower. The weed had so intoxicated Bullock that he did not hear the footsteps of police officers advance on him. They arrested him for diesel theft.

Ezekiel had the rest of previous night's spaghetti for breakfast. He thought of going to buy some foodstuffs. He concluded that Gloria might want to give him another stomach care.

He met Bullock's girlfriend on his way out. She looked gloomy, her eyes swollen from crying. "Madam, you don't look well. What is the matter? Where is Bullock?"

"Bullock is in the police cell. They have arrested him."

"What happened?"

She sat at his veranda and wept, "He was caught while stealing diesel."

"That was Bullock's business?"

She nodded, "yes, but he promised he was going to stop this month."

"You knew and did not try to stop him? Why, madam, what will be the fate of you and your child?"

"I don't know what to do. I am just heartbroken and confused."

"It is okay. Just wipe your tears. Where is your son?"

"He is at my parents' house. I will pick up few of my things to live there for a while."

"Is Bullock aware of this?"

"Yes, he asked me to go to my parents. We will be safer there while I try to get him released from police custody. I need to source for his bail money."

"Okay, go in and pack. I will see you off to the bus stop. Sorry, pull yourself together." He helped her up and she went into her house.

Ezekiel came to the clinic. He enquired about Gloria from the reception. He got a direction to her office. Temba was the first to see him and whispered to Gloria. Rachel cleared her throat.

He strode to Gloria's desk, "Hi, Gloria, good to see you."

"Good day, Ezekiel. Good to see you too."

He recognized Temba from his neighbourhood. "Hello, Temba," he waved at her.

"Hi, Ezekiel." Temba waved at him.

Rachel extended her hand, "Hello handsome. I'm Gloria's roommate and colleague."

He shook her hand, "it's a pleasure to meet you."

"Gloria has told me a lot about you." Rachel said.

For a minute, Ezekiel felt embarrassed. He thought over what Gloria might have discussed with her friends about him, "I hope she didn't say awful things about me, my house or my neighbourhood?" he asked.

Gloria blushed, "Rachel, that's enough. Keep quiet." She smiled at Ezekiel. "I am sorry, Ezekiel. I do not know what to do with that girl. She can be a big bone in my throat. You didn't tell me you were coming to the clinic."

"I thought I'd surprise you and say thank you for the other day," he presented a rose and card to Gloria.

Rachel and Temba fawned over his gesture. Gloria sniffed the flower and blushed. It seemed little stars danced in her eyes.

"Thank you, Ezekiel. It so lovely and smells good." Gloria said.

"And here is what I owe you for my treatment," he gave her an envelope.

Gloria checked the envelope and saw the money she loaned him and an extra tip, "you shouldn't have bothered. Why did you have to?"

"One, a promise is a debt. Two, you rendered a great service to me. Thank you," Ezekiel bowed.

"You are welcome," Gloria blushed and covered her face with the flower.

"Will you mind seeing me off?"

"Oh, I wouldn't mind," Gloria stood and straightened the creases on her uniform. Rachel winked at Gloria. They walked out of the building and into the cool evening atmosphere.

"I saw the look on your face when Rachel was blabbing. I did not say more than I should. Rachel is just a loud mouth that feels she must know everything, especially about my life," Gloria laughed.

"I know. But for a moment I had thought all you chatted to your friends was about my little shack in a shanty."

"Don't be silly. I did no such thing."

"I believe you." He smiled comfily.

"It is surprising your reason for coming was to thank and pay me back. What about your injury?"

"It is fine. It is healing well."

"You mind me checking?"

"I don't mind. But I've got to go."

"Okay, can I come over to your house tomorrow evening?"

"Thank you, I will be grateful."

"I would see you then, bye."

"Bye, Gloria."

Gloria paid Ezekiel a visit. She was attracted to him and needed an excuse to be closer to him. They discussed and laughed over funny remarks. They ate food prepared by Ezekiel.

To fulfil her purpose of the visit, she examined his leg before leaving.

"Thank you for coming."

"It is my pleasure."

"Since my leg has healed nicely, I was thinking of engaging you further."

"Really, you want to see me often?" Gloria was surprised.

"Oh, it's nothing personal."

"Oh." Gloria was disappointed.

"Yes, it would be nice if your team can come to my neighbourhood and register the people for NHIS. We all should benefit from this scheme."

"That's a great idea. But, our clinic does not cover this district."

"Oh."

"Yes, but I would speak with my Director. Let us see if we can work some things out. It would require some few procedures."

"I will be grateful if it pulls through. The health decadence here is awful. The people cannot afford good medication."

"Inferknow needs total environmental operation."

"Let's take it one at a time."

"It is the best measure."

"Yes, how about we have lunch on Saturday?"

"Lunch would be fine. I would prepare it. Your stew was a little salty."

"You didn't tell me."

"I didn't want to offend my host."

"You should have told me. Please, do not deny me the opportunity of improving my culinary skills. I want to be a great Chef!"

Gloria laughed, "Okay, I will, sir."

"Thanks, madam. By the way, I was not planning the lunch in my house. We will eat out."

"That sounds like a date."

"Yes, I want to go on a date with you. I want to spend more time with you too." Ezekiel smiled. He had noticed she liked him. "Gloria, I like you."

Gloria blushed and walked briskly. She hailed a tricycle and entered before Ezekiel reached her. She averted his gaze and faced downward. Her eyes flickered as the tricycle moved. Ezekiel rubbed his face and grinned.

CHAPTER ELEVEN

Chief Daggers and his wife argued over Jerry's death. He tried to calm her but the irate woman vowed to go to the authorities with the truth.

"You are threatening me?"

"It is not a threat. I will have you arrested. You will rot in jail for killing my son." She made for the door and he grabbed her hand off the doorknob. He held her arm tightly and shook her.

"Will you get your hands off me?" She shrugged his hands off her arm.

"I am warning you. You will put your life in danger by doing this." She opened the door and he slammed the door close. Some furniture in the bedroom rattled. He grabbed her shoulder, "listen to me. Do not do this. Please. You do not want to lose your husband as well?"

"Get your hands off me, you monster." She pushed him and he hit his head against a sculpture. She started for the door.

Chief Daggers lifted the sculpture and smashed her head. She slid to the floor and died.

Their two teenage daughters rushed into the bedroom. "Dad, what happened to mom? She is not breathing." They were crying over her.

Chief Daggers staggered towards his wardrobe.

Elizabeth rushed into the bedroom. She saw the bloodied sculpture and guessed he killed her. "Oga, you killed madam!" She began to run outside.

Chief Daggers quickly reached for his silent pistol. He shot Elizabeth three times. His children were surprised. Before they could get out of the shock, Chief Daggers fired a bullet each in their hearts. "Forgive me," he shut his eyes.

In the night, he wrapped their bodies with different wrappers. He put them at the back seat and boot. He drove to a burning dumpsite in Inferknow. He threw each corpse into the inferno and added fuel, "By morning, their bodies would have burned to charcoal." The fire reflected in his eyes as he watched them burn along with the waste.

He drove to Good Evening Street Brothel. Mama was expecting him. She allowed him into her lodge. After undressing him, she gave him a massage and caressed his manhood. He groaned in pleasure and agony.

While he had sex with Mama, he began to weep. His tears dropped on her. She cleaned the tears, "what is the matter?"

"Nothing, just get on me and sex the hell out of me." Mama did as instructed. Chief Daggers stopped crying and sucked the taut nipples dangling in his face.

Chief Daggers did not return to his house for a week. He ate, slept and had sex with Mama. She consoled him whenever he cried.

"You don't want to tell me what the matter is?"

"You have known me for years. I am a man of few words."

Gloria and her team of nurses came to register residents of Inferknow for NHIS. They slashed the registration fee to Five Hundred Naira for adults and made the registration free for children below eighteen year old.

Ezekiel was impressed. He could not take his eyes off Gloria during the whole exercise. He was there to hand her a pen and a bottle of water. At a point, he volunteered to be a photographer; he captured images for the applicants' passport.

After the exercise, Gloria decided to pay her mother a visit. She was close to Good Evening Street, so why not!

Gloria sighed and entered the brothel premises. She dialled a number and put the phone to her ears when the receiver picked the call, "Mama, I am outside. What is your room number?" Mama stuttered on the phone. Gloria cut the dial and stopped Fassa and Gwen.

"Excuse me; please I am here to see Mama. What is her room number?"

Fassa appraised her inquisitively, "And who are you?" She asked.

"I am Gloria, I am Mama's daughter."

"Oh, she is Mama's daughter," Gwen said excitedly.

Fassa pointed to Mama's room. "Thank you," Gloria said. Fassa and Gwen admired her as she walked away.

Gloria knocked on her mother's door. She did not answer the door.

Mama opened it a while later. Chief Daggers came to Mama's side. "He was just leaving," Mama said.

Chief Daggers gave Mama some money, "I might not see you for a long while." Mama collected the money shyly. He left.

Gloria stared at her mother squarely. "Mama, I haven't seen you in a while."

"Come in, how have you been?"

She ate and discussed with Mama. It was late when Gloria left the brothel. She turned down her mother's request to spend the night. It was hard to find a vehicle going uptown. The tricycles refused to journey beyond the suburb of Inferknow. She waited near Protocol's kiosk. He noticed she had been standing for a long time and offered her a bench. Gloria thanked Protocol and sat.

"Did you try to get admitted into the brothel and it was not successful? I can help you get in. I have plenty connection. I will talk to one of the women for you. Mama or Faith will help you," Protocol self-importantly said.

"No, thanks, I will leave." Gloria called Ezekiel on the phone and he agreed to accommodate her for the night. She took a tricycle to his house.

Ezekiel waited for her at the bus stop. He took her bag when she descended from the tricycle. "I thought you had gone home," he said.

"No, I stopped by to visit my mother. She lives around here."

"Wow, that's nice. You should have told me. I would love to meet her."

"Let us go, I am starting to catch cold." Gloria quickly said to detract the topic.

"Yes, I am sorry. Let us go." They walked to his house in silence. Ezekiel noticed Gloria was unease and thought that perhaps she did not have a pleasant time with her mother.

"I will prepare tea; there are biscuits in the fridge."

"I had dinner at my mother's."

"Really, then I don't understand. You should have slept in your mother's house. It is very late."

"I thought I could get home. But no vehicle was boarding uptown."

"That's okay. I am glad you called me. It can be horrific out here."

"Ezekiel, that's enough please. What I saw was horrific enough."

"What do you mean?"

"Just forget about it, Ezekiel. Did I make a mistake by coming to your house?"

Ezekiel put his hands up. "At least have a bath."

Gloria refused to have a bath. "You could at least wash your face and feet," he insisted. She nodded and stood. He led her to the bathroom. Ezekiel waited with a small towel. "Here, use it to dry up. It is a new towel. I have never used it."

"Thank you." Gloria took it and wiped her face with the towel. She inhaled the factory fragrance of the towel.

Gloria slept on the bed while Ezekiel napped on the couch. There was a heavy breeze, and the curtain slightly opened. He awakened. He could see Gloria sleeping peacefully. She rolled on the bed and he was afraid she might fall. He dropped the comforter and two pillows on the floor by the bedside. In case Gloria tumbled, she would have a soft landing.

CHAPTER TWELVE

In the morning, Gloria woke, stretched her arms, and yawned loudly. Ezekiel opened his eyes, "Good morning, Gloria."

"Good morning, Ezekiel," she heard sounds from the busy neighbourhood. "What time is it?"

"It is almost eight o'clock."

"Oh my, I overslept. Ezekiel, why didn't you wake me up?" She jumped out of the bed and began wearing her sandals. Ezekiel seeing she was in a hurry, dashed out of the house. He returned. She was trying to brush her hair with his hairbrush. Ezekiel chuckled.

"What is funny?" She cleaned her face with a baby wipe.

"Nothing," he moved closer to her, too close to her, "here, have this."

"What is that?"

"It is menthol sweet. I know in such a hurry, you may not want to brush your teeth. No motorist will carry you with a foul mouth odour."

"Indeed," she collected the sachet, popped three tablets into her mouth, and chewed quickly. "Hmmm," she inhaled and exhaled. She smelt her fresh breath and smiled. "Fresh, I will keep the rest." She put the sachet of menthol sweet in her jean pocket.

"Don't mention."

"Move aside," Ezekiel moved out of her way and she picked up her bag. "Thank you, Ezekiel. I have to rush home, have my bath and go to work. Thanks." She pecked him on the lips and walked out of the house. She paused at the doorstep and glanced back at Ezekiel; she blushed and ran out of the house.

"You are welcome." He said dreamily. Ezekiel touched his lips, "you are welcome, any time." He fell on the bed and luxuriated in the past moment. He reminiscence the kiss and clutched his chest with joy.

Protocol was riding his bicycle. He stopped when he saw Gloria come out in her dishevelled appearance from Ezekiel's house. He posed with one leg on the wheel and grinned. "Smart girl, she found a way to make the money, after all," he said. Gloria walked pass him. "Hey, sissy," Gloria reluctantly stopped and looked at him, "hello, you don't recognize me? I gave you my bench to sit on last night."

"Oh you, now I remember. Thank you. I appreciate."

He looked serious, "I didn't know you were mobile, you would have just followed me to my house and given to me what you fed Ezekiel last night. Looking at you, I am sure you had one for the road, eh?" Protocol clapped and smirked.

Gloria got angry and flogged his face with her handbag. She humped and stepped on his foot. He howled. She pushed his bicycle and he clattered to the ground with his wares. Gloria grinned wickedly and stormed off.

Ezekiel heard the clock ding-dong, "Oh, gosh, I am late for work." He was out of bed in a flash and went to the bathroom. Someone was bathing in the bathroom and singing loudly. Ezekiel moved close to the gutter, he brushed his teeth, washed his face and feet. He hurried to his room, sprayed some cologne and hurried to work.

Ezekiel picked up Gloria from work and they went in a taxi to a restaurant. They had jollof rice, chicken and salad. They cuckolded and fed each other.

After the meal, he took her hand. "Come, Gloria. There is a cool garden behind the restaurant. Let us enjoy the fresh air."

He led her to a swing. He made her sit on the chair and started swinging her. Gloria relaxed in it and watched Ezekiel, each swing forward brought her close enough to perceive his breath. She reached for her phone with one hand and this caused her to slip. Ezekiel lunged at the oncoming swing and caught her.

Gloria shuddered. "Are you okay?" he asked. She nodded against his chest. "I am glad you did not fall." A romantic song swerved into the garden. They stared desirously into one another's eyes. Their hearts beat fast. Gloria traced Ezekiel's lips with her hand. He moved his hands down to her waist and hugged her tight.

She nuzzled into his body. She thought his arms were so secure. She caressed his shoulder. He held her chin and gently pushed her face so he could stare into her eyes. Her stare was unwavering. He bent his head and kissed her. Gloria was ready, she kissed him with pent up passion. They kissed for ten minutes.

"I have wanted to do this for so long." He said.

"Why did it take you this long?"

"I wasn't sure how you felt about me." He raised her hand and kissed it. "I didn't know how you would react if I hug and kiss you. I am glad you responded beautifully." His eyes fell to her heaving bosom. He kissed her again. Her hardened nipples grazed his chest and he groaned.

He slowly lowered her on the lawn while kissing her. They smooched and kissed. He stopped kissing her, Gloria moaned in disapproval. "Sweetheart, if we don't stop, I might just take you on this garden bed," said Ezekiel.

"Then take me, sweetie. I need you." She bent his head lower and kissed him.

"Baby, I need you too. But this is a public place. Someone can walk in here and see us." She sighed frustratingly. "Come, let me take you home." He lifted her into his arms, walked through the restaurant, and put her down when they were outside. He hired a taxi that took them to Gloria's house. Ezekiel paid the cabman and he zoomed off.

"Why didn't you tell him to wait? He should have taken you home."

"That would have meant a round fare."

"Would you accept I pay for the fare? He has not driven far. Look, he is stuck in traffic."

"I would not accept the money from you. Why are you bothered? I will just take a bus and save the return cab fare for another dinner date." Gloria's eyes glowed. Ezekiel nodded and smiled. They fixed a dinner date at Ezekiel's house for the next weekend.

Rachel keenly watched Gloria dress up. She was smiling smugly when Gloria turned around.

"What?" Gloria asked.

"The dress, the perfume, and the smile," Rachel walked towards her.

"Go away," Gloria threw a scarf at her.

"Hey, I just want to adjust your bra strap," she adjusted both so that the straps cupped Gloria's breasts perfectly. "There you go, now he wouldn't be able to take his eyes off you."

"He is just a friend."

"Yes, I know," Rachel pecked Gloria on the cheek, "You look so beautiful. Your friend must be special?"

"Stop being too nosy, I left some food in the kitchen. Please do not forget to lock the door when I leave. Do not wait up for me. I will use my key to get in."

"Yes, grandma," Rachel drawled.

Ezekiel had a visitor. "Guy, it will be very cheap for you to put her in the house. Do you not know her mother is one of the oldest prostitutes in Good Evening Brothel? My friend and I have even had her on two occasions." Charles said.

Ezekiel had not discussed personal issues with Gloria, so he was surprised at this information. "Wow you don't mean it. You mean Gloria is a daughter of a woman with easy virtues?"

Charles did a snake twist with his hand, "Easy pay, and easy access."

Gloria had been standing at the door. She wanted to knock but decided against that when she heard Ezekiel and his friend's conversation.

"So guy, you don't have to pay a dime as dowry. Do you want to call on her mother at the brothel for formal introduction or the marriage because I am sure she does not know her father? That's if the mother knows who impregnated her," Charles chortled. Gloria bit her lips.

"So my man, just impregnate her and she will pack her baggage into your house."

Blinded in tears, Gloria ran away. Her lower lip was bleeding. She did not hear Ezekiel defend how he would do the honourable things by her and gave credit to her mother for raising such a decent woman despite her environment and profession. He said he would be proud to have such a woman as his mother-in-law.

Gloria did not know that soon after she left, Ezekiel walked his friend out of his house. He warned Charles never to cross his threshold again. She did not know the last thought on Ezekiel's mind was to work harder and get them all out of the slum. He vowed to get Mama out of Good Evening Brothel. He made a personal pact that he would only see her when he had secured a good paying job.

CHAPTER THIRTEEN

Joel took shots of Lillian with his phone's camera and they had rounds of selfie together in the park. He pursued her around a small mat and they dropped exhausted onto the lawn, their faces were inches apart. Her beautiful smile captivated Joel. Spellbound by her deep throaty laughter, Joel laughed almost insanely and went grave silent.

She called out his name when he did not say a word. Her soft voice enthralled Joel, something akin to the way he felt with Faith. He kept quiet so that she called out his name repeatedly. He took her hand when she tried to stand up and go look for him.

"Oh, you are here. I was worried because of the silence."

"I'm here."

"I thought you had gone..."

"No, let's go from here. It's getting chilly and I left your shawl in the car." He gently took her hand.

Mrs Lawson was angry when she saw her son in company of Lillian. She had come there with other party members for a meeting. She felt threatened on seeing the way Joel lovingly guided Lillian out of the park. It was her plan to get Joel remarried as soon as possible in order to form a great alliance before the primary elections.

Mrs Lawson excused herself from the crew. "I will be damned if I allow another low class girl come to ruin all my efforts." She said and angrily walked towards them.

"Joel, who is she?"

Joel was shocked to see his mother in front of him. She stood with hands on her waist. He said the first words that came to his mind. "Mom, are you stalking me?"

"Joel, I asked you a question. Who is she?"

"I would be back." Joel walked Lillian to the car. He guided her to sit at the back and left the door open.

"Lillian, I just want to have some moment with my mom. I will be back shortly, okay?" Lillian nodded and smiled. He patted her hand and left.

Joel got into an intense argument with his mother. She saw him with Lillian and concluded they were in a relationship and she vehemently kicked against it.

"Have you gone mad? What were you thinking? You really want an engagement with a low class blind girl. Another bat, Did you forget what it was like with your father?"

"That is not the case with Lillian. My father was in his early eighties when his eyesight started to fail because of age-related macular degeneration. He had lost all central vision in both eyes before his death."

"And you know I couldn't put up with your father in that whole frustrated year, so why do you want to mess me up with this girl for a daughter-in-law?"

"Mom, don't start, please we can't go on talking about it. The issue is settled. I will do whatever my heart desires. Lillian is my fiancée and I am making her my wife soon. You keep talking about class, class, class all the time. Class is not about money and societal status you know. It's about character and the good state of one's heart."

"You won't cease to amaze me. Out of the million girls out there, the one you deemed fit to be my daughter-in-law is a blind girl. Get this girl out of your interest, I shall find you a suitable wife. How inconsiderate can you be, son? Have you thought of how we will cope with her disabilities?"

"There are abilities in disabilities, mom. Aside losing her vision, Lillian is a fully-grown beautiful woman that can take care of herself. Besides, we have countless house cleaners at home. She wasn't born blind you know, so there is every tendency of her seeing again."

"And until then we have to slave ourselves for her? Wash her panties, bath her, feed her, and change her sanitary towel and what else?"

"Stop it, mom, I've said Lillian can handle all that. You are over exaggerating. My dad was responsible for himself despite being blind, it is not like you slaved anything for his health sake." He raised a hand. "Let us be, mom. Please."

"No! You must retract that decision. Take back your proposal. I will not have you bring misery upon our family. I will not let you. It would be over my dead body."

"Then so be it, mom. My mind is certain on what I want. I shall proceed to buy another house. I need to breathe freely. Excuse me."

"My son, how dare you defy your mother for a woman?"

"She is not just any woman. She is my heartthrob, the one my heart beats for, my future wife, the mother of my unborn kids. I love Lillian and nothing is going to stop our union." He walked out on his mother.

"Oh, I see! Okay then, bring her in and we shall see if both of you descended this earth before me. We shall see."

Joel and Ezekiel met in the park. "What happened to you, you weren't limping the last time I saw you." Joel said to Ezekiel.

"I had another accident at work. Little accidents will not be the death of me. The scars they leave behind are countless. The last injury was bad. I'm glad Gloria came around to help me heal faster."

"Hmmm, Ezy my main man, I see you are in love. I have not seen you blush. Gloria must be magic. How is she? I cannot wait to meet her. I am sorry. I am in a web of problems. I'll see her soon."

"She's great. Something came up and I've decided I won't see her for a while."

"You decided? This means she is not aware you would not be seeing her soon."

"Yes." He thought of Gloria's long absence and said, "But strangely she hasn't bothered to call or come see me. It is odd. We were supposed to have dinner and she did not show up. I was thinking she stayed away because she wants me to save my little money. You see, on our last date, we argued over taxi fare." He narrated the scene.

"Hope she is fine?"

"Yes, she is. Temba, the secretary in the same clinic she works, lives in my neighbourhood, so she told me Gloria is doing well."

"It is strange she has not come to see you. Gloria had grown fond of you. Ezy, I think you should go and see her."

"Yes, I'll, but until I get a good job."

"Yes, that reminds me. I will involve you in a business. We can go into partnership. Come to the office on Monday and we will work something out." Ezekiel thanked him and they shook hands.

"Your mom called; she was mad as hell. You do not intend marrying Lillian do you? Can you cope with her kind of woman and what about Faith?"

"Is Lillian less of a human being? Well, she already lives with me. Her foster mother lives in my house too. Soon, I will register Lillian in the Art and Vision Centre. I am not going to marry Lillian. I just said all that to infuriate my mom, that woman annoys me to the core."

"Joel, Joel, see I don't like when you sound about your mother like this, I don't like it one bit."

"She screamed murder when she saw us together at the park. She assumed I was going to marry Lillian. I felt like kicking that woman's chin."

"That's enough man, you talk too stupid sometimes."

"She is always out to ruin my life. I lost Faith because of her. Have you forgotten so soon? Ezekiel, she did not allow me enjoy my marriage from the first day. What kind of mother charms her son into a drunk because she was dissatisfied with his choice of a wife? I always made love with my wife in a drunken state. I virtually raped her in the madness my mother sown in me. She always talked about class. Faith was a damn nobody to her; she did not fit into my mother's socio-political class. My happiness meant nothing to her."

"Ease man, that's all in the past."

Joel turned his back to Ezekiel. "My past has come to haunt me. You saw it too; it stared straight into my face. I live in a nightmare."

Silence echoed around them until Ezekiel broke it, "are you sure you've not fallen in love with this woman."

He faced him. "A man, who is on the ground, is not scared of any fall. He can't fall."

"He can, he can lay flat on the ground, and that's the greatest fall ever. He may not break his nose, but he can get dirty by the mud or dust from the ground."

"Don't worry about me."

"Joel, are you growing romantic feelings for Lillian?"

"No, I'm not."

"If I didn't know you better, I would have said you were telling the truth." Joel looked coldly at Ezekiel.

CHAPTER FOURTEEN

Joel called up Faith and pleaded to have dinner with her. She declined because it was the hour of business. She later settled for lunch after much persuasion. Faith went to Mama's room to use her full dressing mirror.

"Faith, if he wants you back in his life, why don't you just forget this hustle and move on with your better half and have a more fulfilling life?"

"Believe me Mama; a life with him is hell. I saw hell from his mother. Joel in his weakness could not protect me from prejudice. I suffered, Mama, I really went through the toughest period of my life. Losing my parents and sister in a car crash was not as hurtful as my six-month-old marriage."

"But you still love him," Mama said agitatedly.

Faith applied Mama's red lipstick to her lips and clamped her lips for perfection. "I'd rather not discuss love. Mama, you convinced me to meet him once; I am solely doing this for you. Love does not exist in my world. I doubt if it was present in my union. I am just lost to lust. Joel's driver is waiting downstairs for me. I should leave."

Faith picked up her purse and assured Mama she would be back before the start of business. Mama sighed, and wished the couple would set things right and be happy in their relationship. She opened the Bible application on her phone and searched for chapters she had jotted down in Bible Study.

Every Thursday was her day off for worship and praise day in church. She ignored a call from Chief Daggers who had insistently booked a rendezvous with her for today. Mama switched off her phone on the third ring and concentrated on her study.

Joel sat with an untouched pack of juice in his front. He looked up from his phone. The sight of Faith mesmerised him. He intensely followed her steps with desirous longing in his eyes. He cursed himself for remaining silent when his mother had made him choose between her and Faith.

Faith had taken his prolonged silence, in the heated moment to mean he would stick with his maternal relationship. She had sent her wedding band and divorce paper through courier the following week. The documents had remained unsigned and his love never wavered. Joel wished Faith would give him another chance to choose a lifetime with her and make things right.

"Oh, damn my stupidity," this time, he cursed aloud.

"Hi." Faith sat before Joel fully stood to draw out the seat for her.

"How're you?"

"I am fine." She answered without looking at him and unlocked her phone.

"Won't you ask how I am doing?"

"You look great as always."

"But on the inside, I am so messed up."

Faith looked away from the instant pain that came into his eyes. "Joel, please, I've not come here to discuss your personal problems. You promised me we would only have a hitch free lunch. Now, before I forget, let me have the payment for my time. A deal is a deal, dear client."

"Here, I will always keep to my bargain." He put a white envelope in her outstretched hand.

"I know how well you keep to a bargain." Faith opened the envelope of Fifty Thousand Naira and found an ATM card within.

"Hey waiter," Joel snapped his fingers at a nearby attendant. He placed an order for their favourite meal.

"And what is this?" She flipped the card in her hand.

"I want to have more lunch dates with you. The pin is 0235. You have your payments in advance and you can cash out at any time."

"How many instalments do I have in this account?"

"You have a lifetime instalment." Faith hissed and deposited the card in her purse. She was sure a fortune rested in the bank account.

"You can have my juice while we wait for our meal. Did you notice I called for our favourite?"

"Yes, thank you. It has been long I had it. I missed the aroma and taste."

The truth of her statement hurt Joel. His resolve to give her every luxurious treat and stand by her grew fierce. Faith did not hesitate when he clasped her hands in his. Faith loosened her guard and relaxed in his warmness.

'What will it hurt if he is on her customer's list?' Faith thought as he massaged her wrist and knuckles, which sent waves of pleasures to her nipples.

Faith ended up having a wonderful time with Joel. They relieved in some safe moments of their courtship and laughed off some naughty past events. Joel took her on a long evening drive around the lightened city with beautiful streetlights and life. Faith forgot about Good Evening Street for the moment and melted in the gentlemanliness of Joel.

Faith had thought Joel would try to kiss her before they parted, but he had painstakingly resisted the urge. The man she knew would not have let her go without a peck as they had done in their past numerous dates. However, she remembered this was their present. Joel must have read her mind, but he did not oblige her fantasy. He wanted her to take that longing with her; he wanted the questions in her mind to bring her back to him for answers.

Faith refused to accompany him to pick up Lillian from the Art and Vision Centre. Joel sent her off with the driver and walked the short distance to the three-storey building.

CHAPTER FIFTEEN

They had another lunch date. Joel revealed he never signed the divorce paper, so in the eyes of the law, they were still man and wife. Faith punched him repeatedly on the chest. She was angry he made her commit adultery all these while. If he wanted to stay married to her, why had he not stopped her from leaving or come to look for her all these past months.

She hit Joel and said, "You didn't do me a favour by keeping your signature from that paper. You dirtied me. All these while I thought my only waywardness was banging for money, now, I come to know I have been a shameless adulterer. How do you expect me to be elated at this news of still being your wife? How will you have me back on our matrimonial bed? I must look repulsive to you. What do you really want from me? What?"

Joel held her hands, "I need you in my life." He assured her he wanted her as his soul mate and back home.

She turned her face away. "Please take me home. I've to get ready for business." Joel's lips switched in anger when she referred to the brothel as home.

In drunken state, a man forced a female waiter to sit on his thighs; this was against the hotel policy. They did not mix pleasure with business; the servants were to attend customers' filial needs, while the whores were in charge of carnal satisfaction. A fight broke out between the drunken man and the club bouncer. Joel hurried out of the hotel with Faith. He took her up the brothel stairs and into her room.

More than ever, Joel was weary of Faith's adamant decision to remain in the brothel. He dragged the frilly clothe she was about to change into for the night. Joel warned her that if she wore the dress and went down to hustle for the night, he was going to walk out of her life and never return. Faith's heart skipped. Joel did not wait to hear her retort, he dropped the dress on her bed and walked away.

Faith wondered if he would wait downstairs and dare her to appear. She looked through the window and saw him drive his car out of the driveway. She clutched the curtain to her chest and wished Joel would repeat those stern words to her again.

Joel did not know she had stopped prostituting since he appeared in her life. The first client he had seen her with, was her last. Seeing Joel that day, she could not put up her acts together.

At home, Joel helped Lillian unpacked some items out of her box. He saw a silver necklace and took it. He raised it and saw it had a locket. Out of curiosity, he opened the locket and gasped.

"Joel, I hope you are not having a hard time unpacking my stuff. You do not have to bother. Mom Tricia will help when she returns from the market."

"No, no Lillian. I am glad I unpacked this luggage." He put the necklace in his back pocket. "Sit," he guided her to sit on the bed and smiled. Lillian smiled appreciatively.

CHAPTER SIXTEEN

"Rachel, I have a feeling you shouldn't go out tonight. I do not know why I have had this strong conviction all day. I think you should stay home tonight."

"Gloria, you don't know what you're saying. I am about to hit it very big. This Chief is a big shot. Just to thank me for coming the other day, he gave me Three Hundred Thousand Naira cash, and he credited my account with Seven Hundred Thousand Naira. Babe that's one million we are talking."

"Stay home tonight, Rachel, I beg you."

"No girl. I need money for my Master Degree, which is the more reason I have to gather some more money. Gloria mommy, I am out of here. Pray for me. I have to go get ready for my dinner with Chief." She wriggled her waist and left the living room.

Gloria thought sadly on why Rachel was this materialistic. "Forgive me Rachel. I need to do this," she dialled a number from her mobile phone.

Faith came home with Joel. They were talking. Lillian froze in her tracks. The voice was familiar. It was her sister. She screamed '*Faith.*' Faith recognized her lost sister in a second. She ran to her side and paused.

"Lillian." She paused for her to meet her half way. Faith expected Lillian to run into her open arms. "What happened to you, you're not excited to see me?" She faintly asked.

"I would run into your arms if I knew the spot you're standing right now, sister. My lovely sister...My senses are yet to know people by their steps." Faith looked closer into the still eyeballs of Lillian.

Joel talked from behind them, "Last night, I came across your family album in Lillian's locket. I knew straight away that she was the lost sister you thought had died. I could not wait for dawn to get to you. I decided to surprise you, I am glad you came with me."

Faith turned to Joel. "She is the lady you wanted me to accompany and pick up the other day?" At Joel's nod, she gathered Lillian into her arms and hugged her very tight. "How did my spirit reject a chance to be reunited with my sister? Joel, Joel you should have told me it was my sister."

He laughed. "How was I supposed to know she was your sister?"

"Somehow you should have known; she looks like me. The mention of her name would have possibly made my heart ask some questions."

"Forgive me," he said in mock apology.

"Oh, don't be silly." She sniffed. "Thank you Joel, you brought my sister into my life by way of destiny. You led her in paths that have restored our lost hope of ever finding each other. Thank you Joel, we shall be her light. All our crooked moments, our imperfect moments, from today onward we will strengthen our love and our bond will be strong forever." The three of them hugged one another.

Rachel got to Prime Royal Hotel and went straight to Chief Dagger's room.

"Chief…" She ran into his arms as soon as he answered the door.

"My baby, welcome, welcome, what took you so long? I thought you weren't going to see me today."

"Haba Chief Daggers." She caressed his cheeks.

He pecked her soundly on her cheeks. "So I thought my baby."

"I'm here, how could I have missed a meeting with you, eh? I stopped by my favourite boutique to get me some nice sexy wear, hot lingerie just for you." She pecked him.

"That's my baby, so when do I see it?"

"Just relax while I go freshen up. Lie down and stay hot for me my baby."

Rachel went into the bathroom to have a quick shower. Chief Daggers had insisted they would not use condom. She did not want to have any argument on the bed so she inserted a female condom. After sex, she went back to the bathroom to wash. To her shock, she found a live scorpion in the sac. She covered her mouth to block the scream. She breathed to keep calm.

The brown scorpion' pincer squeal and its elongated body shrank. Rachel imagined how the stinger would have entered her body and circulated toxins in her system. She did not know Chief Daggers was a venomous human being that could cause lethal damage to a fellow human. She had heard stories of rituals, but she never dreamed it could be her fate. She crushed the scorpion with a fire extinguisher and a scream came from the room.

Rachel rushed in to see Chief Daggers was dead. She was hysterical. She quickly dressed up and picked up her phone that had been ringing.

"Hi Rachel, it is Mike. I saw you walk into Prime Royal Hotel. I wondered if I could have a glimpse of you."

"Mike, where are you?"

"I'm at the lobby."

"Please, meet me at the fourth floor."

"Are you okay? Rachel you sound so scared. Is anything the matter?"

"Please quit asking many questions and come immediately."

"Okay, I'm on my way."

"Okay, be quick." Rachel ended the call. She breathed. "Rachel, just calm down." She packed her belongings and scanned the room. She nodded and dashed out.

Rachel met Mike at the elevator area. They walked hand in hand out of the hotel like lovers. She trembled when they reached the car park and Mike hugged her. He said some words to sooth her but Rachel was nervous. He peered at her face and saw how panicky she was, her teeth were clattering. Mike thought she was in great shock and decided they leave the scene. He removed his jacket and wore it on her sleeveless short gown. "Come, let's take you home."

Mike called Gloria on their way. Gloria dropped the phone and slumped into a chair. Mama rushed forward and sat next to her. She narrated what had happened between Rachel and the same Chief she knew. Mama opened her mouth and shook her head in dismay.

The moment Mike brought Rachel into the house; she fell on the floor and cried. Mama pulled her up to sit and cuddled her. Gloria stood against the wall, still in shock. Mike bid them goodnight and let himself out.

CHAPTER SEVENTEEN

The government had inspected the neighbourhood. Its decision was to modernize the degrading physical structure, which would ultimately overturn moral decadence of the inhabitants. INFERKNOW had owned up to the status of a highly sociable neighbourhood gritty by more brothels harbouring teenage prostitutes and miscreants. The project was to upgrade the roads with inter-locking stones, organised motor parks, road beautification and a sub-hub of decent people and businesses.

The demolition of the disorganized part of the territory brought relief to a lot of people and decent companies. The government wanted to expand its road. Good Evening Street encroached into its plan. This affected the hotel and brothel. The bulldozers would not spare a block. They gave a date for residents to evacuate the buildings for subsequent demolition. Gloria brought a van to pack up Mama's belongings to live with her.

Gloria and Mama's savings pulled together, they were able to open a provision store. Mama could not help but flirt with her male customers and admirers.

"Mama, why make it look like a bad decision that I brought you to live with me? Mama, please you have to stop these flirtations, people are beginning to raise eyebrows and point fingers at us. People are already connecting you with Good Evening Street due to your constant association with that man called Protocol, who now owns a kiosk in front of Meddling Town Square Company. Please stay away from the gateman, he narrates to anybody that cares to know how life on Good Evening Street was. Mama, how can you be smoking in your own shop? You have three ashtrays here. This will definitely scare away responsible people to patronize your store."

"Gloria, don't talk down on me like I'm your child. You should have let me go live in another neighbourhood where I had already paid two years rent for an apartment, before you forced me to come live in your house."

"Mama, whatever but please, do not bring any form of prostitution to this neighbourhood." Gloria clamped her mouth the moment those words slipped out.

Mama's eyes became fiery. "Hey girl, I would have my respect. I would have my respect no matter what, so watch your tongue. This prostitution, I getting laid almost every night had put food in your belly, put clothes over your body and paid your school fees when you were young."

Gloria knelt before her mother. "I know Mama. Mama, I have come a bit far to making it, by God we are making it. Let me feed you too with my own labour. Would you have preferred I feed you with money I'm paid after being laid by nameless men?"

"No my daughter, I'm happy the way my daughter had turned out. I never ceased to pray for a good upbringing for you. It was not by my powers, the living God I serve made you stand out of that squalor. I am grateful you stood by the morals I taught you, despite lacking the simplest of it. I was never a good model to you."

"Then make me proud, and be good, Mama. Do not bring shame upon us, mom, please. Go get ready; first church service is always fresh for the soul." She hugged her mother.

Mrs Lawson placed a pillow on Lillian's face; the sleepy blind woman woke up.

Lillian sniffed her perfume, "Mother, what? You would try to kill me?"

"Yes, and don't call me mother, I can't birth such a despicable creature."

"Why Mrs Lawson, why, what have I done that you'll carry out such a gruesome act on me? You hatched such a fate on me for what gains."

"It's because you will be the ruin of me and I don't want that to happen."

"But, but I'm not a threat to you."

"Of course you're."

"Me," Lillian touched her bosom.

"Yes you." She dragged her up from the couch with a malicious look on her face. "You will take up your miserable self, and flee this city. I don't want to ever see you around my son again."

"Where will I go? My family is here now. Here is home."

"I see, so you really want to stay with my son forever. You want to be his wife."

"No ma. Joel is like a brother and my guardian angel."

"Why don't you just die and meet your host of angels in heaven? Please leave my son alone, girl."

"Please, don't send me away."

"Lillian, and of what good will staying here be? You want to stay and cast darkness over my son's life with your blindness." Lillian shook her head. Mrs Lawson hissed and stepped on her toes. Lillian yelped in pain. She sneered and went to fix herself a brandy from Joel's bar.

An hour later, Lillian joined Mrs Lawson in the kitchen. She stood at the door, "I came to do some of the chores, and I see you want to cook. Can I assist you in cooking?"

"With which eyes would you use to accomplish that task? Please do not come and complicate my duties for me. Just get out of my sight before I sweep dirt into your face. Get out." Lillian reeled back in fear and almost fell down. Joel arrived on time to catch her.

"Mother, you do not have to be so harsh on her. Where is your humanly instinct for goodness sake? Mom, you should not put an obstacle before the blind. Fear God, mom, be God fearing. She is only blind, not broken, or maimed for life."

"Welcome home son, I've been waiting for you. I have come to your house to tell you, you have five more days to decide, or else you will bury me soon. It is not late for you to change your decision about marrying this bat."

Faith entered the kitchen. "It is too late, dear...mother-in-law." Mrs Lawson was stunned speechless.

CHAPTER EIGHTEEN

"We are from Inferknow high police command; we have an arrest warrant for Miss Rachel Charles."

Gloria rushed out of the kitchen, dusting her hand on the apron. "For what offence, what crime has she committed?" Gloria startlingly asked.

"She is under arrest for the murder of Chief Daggers. Miss Rachel, you should remain silent, anything you say may be used against you in the court of law." Rachel took steps backward. "Miss, just submit yourself for the arrest, cooperate with us, it would be wise and better for you." The police officer opened a handcuff.

Mama rushed into the house and pushed Rachel outstretched hands. "No, let her go. I killed Chief Daggers."

"What, no," Gloria was stunned.

"Mama, no," Rachel held Mama's hand.

"Yes, Chief Daggers was my client. He wanted to use me for rituals; but he died instead. That served him right."

"No Mama, you did not." Rachel said.

"Officers, here is your culprit." Mama stretched her hands.

Gloria pleaded. "Mom, please don't do this."

The police marched Mama out into their waiting van. Gloria fell to the ground and cried. A speechless Rachel just stared after the vehicle.

"Rachel, I want my mom back. Did you see her frightened look when the police led her away like a criminal? My mom might be the worst of women but she doesn't deserve to suffer for another's crime."

"I am sorry Gloria, so sorry for all the pains I'm putting your family through. I will get your mother out of there, I promise. I just wish I listened to you on that day, none of these would have happened."

"You never listened Rachel, my words were noise in your ears, not once did you try to filter it to get some truth out of it."

Mama did not regret her decision. She climbed onto the police van with only one burden, the sadness of getting away from the girls. Mama thought she might not make it to heaven, her Thursday devotions were not enough to earn her a place in that beautiful place. Purgatory may have a cosy shanty for her.

Rachel wanted to console her friend but Gloria's icy command for her to stay away stopped her. She could not stand her mother's exit.

Gloria ran into the house and shut the door. She slowly slid to the floor and wept. Rachel did not go into the house; she intended to walk all night and really get to know the overbearing city she had treaded incautiously. A city that had changed her from the conventional girl she used to be, one taste of the city's fine wine, she had been lost to its barrel of drunkenness.

Mama's damnation dazed Gloria. Just when Mama was ready to turn a pure page in her life, destiny would not let her resolution be great. Gloria asked God if the fulfilment of having a normal life was too much for him to bless her family. In her anger, she went into her shared bedroom with Mama and toppled her mother's praying items. The anointing oil bottle crashed and splattered on the floor.

Gloria rigidly stepped on the bottles that pierced her feet. She shouted to the roof that heaven had not been benevolent to her and Mama. Mama's pregnancy caused grave stigmatization. It was either people called Mama, a prostitute or they called her the daughter of a loosed woman. Gloria dealt with the mockery in silence until she was old enough to retaliate in words and actions for her mother's defence.

This situation forced Gloria into adulthood at a tender age. She began to work odd jobs after school to save enough money to alleviate their status, so that she and Mama could leave the squalor behind. However, she never gathered a substantial amount. She failed her Secondary School Certificate Examination due to lack of preparation.

It took lots of threat from her mother before Gloria diligently wrote her examination. She closed her mind to the fact that her mother used prostitution money to train her through Navy school; her only consolation was that she was going to make enough money one day and help Mama to a reputable standard.

Many times, Gloria had witnessed Mama's distress. Even when she was too ill to walk, she would stand in the cold and wait on her customers. She had once talked her mother into letting her trade off her body as well. For that utterance, Mama had for the first time, severely raised her hands on Gloria. Mama had put her hand on her head; she made Gloria promise she would never lie with a man except for love.

Gloria crawled onto the bed with her bloodied feet and crimson eyes. She slept off with heavy turmoil in her heart, wishing she would wake a happy child with a stable home. She groped for her mother in a darkened cell.

Joel came to see his mother. The police arrested her and other cult members in a shrine with mutilated human bodies. He did not want to come; Faith had coaxed him to get a lawyer for her. However, he went alone.

"Just look at the class you are now. You grope at noonday, today is your doomsday."

"Joel, please get me out of here, son. Honestly, I don't know but your refusal to marry our party chairman's daughter drove me to do all that."

"How? You know I'm not a pity party to dirty political games."

Mrs Lawson stamped her foot on the floor. "But it is the truth, son. I had no other choice since I would not get the backings of the chairperson. I had to look for an alternative." She opened her eyes very wide.

With a look of disgust, Joel spoke. "You need to see how unfit you look behind bars. Okay wait, I should call your maids to bring your great dressing mirror for you to take a long, good look at yourself?" Mrs Lawson cried bitterly. "I guess no, it's a no, right, mom, I shouldn't call the low class people to see their madam in a damned palace? Yes, this palace is despicable, damn despicable. I feel so suffocated in your presence." He banged the cell rods with his hands and did not feel any hurt.

"I promise you son, I only brought the babies as instructed."

"And what did you think was going to be done to a day old babies in such a dark coven? They will take them into wonderful foster homes, really mom?" He rubbed his hair in mix anger and confusion on what to do. Joel walked away; he shut his heart to his mother's alarming call to come back and save her.

An inmate called out to his IPO to get a pastor to deliver him. He asked him in pidgin if his case was normal, that a person that stole a wrap of fufu with cash in his pocket needed spiritual deliverance and not locked up in the cell. The man begged for release out of jail. He claimed his uncle manipulated him to be useless.

CHAPTER NINETEEN

In the morning, when they came face to face, Gloria blankly looked at Rachel. When she finally spoke to Rachel, it was not the tone of her usual sisterly love. Her heart, reserved contempt for what Rachel had caused her mother.

"I wish you had listened to me and stayed back that night. I wish you did not have to be the reason my mother is in jail and going to die. I know my mom is not the best of humans but she does not deserve death by hanging for another's crime. Just when the sun was about to rise in our lives, you overshadowed it, and it is so shocking. I never thought you would be the cause of my most grievous fall in life. Rachel, how can you live with yourself knowing you did this to me?"

Rachel stuttered and tried to touch Gloria, "no, don't try to speak, not another word. I know it is not your fault, and I am not blaming you. Believe me; I hold no grudges against you. But you must understand that now, I hate you." Rachel stifled a cry. "I loathe your voice, and face, please try not to speak with me ever again. I wish you were never a part of my life; I wish we had never crossed path."

By Evening, Rachel had packed all her suitcases. She stood in front of Gloria's door to say goodbye. Two step to get to her side; Rachel saw photographs of the two of them, torn into pieces. She choked on her tears and quickly retreated. She breathed heavily and rested her back against the wall.

Once she regained composure, she patted her face and dropped a tape recorder on the table. She carried their picture. She caught a tear before it slipped to the frame. Rachel looked at Gloria's room one last time and left the house.

All the dreams they had of being best friends forever, Mama sharing her motherly love in-between their homes in the future, to take care of their babies had been shattered. Rachel knew she would be the murderer of Mama; she carried the burden of being the cause of two deaths.

Mama forbade her to take the blames, Mama had said she deserved to be free and have longer years to enjoy a good life, but she would pass the little she had in strangling breath, and she saw it as a way to atone for her sins.

After she left, Gloria found the tape. She sat on the floor and put it to play. Rachel's voice came on.

'Gloria, people had always seen our friendship as extraordinary, the closeness, and the confidence we have in each other (she chuckles). The matron once called me aside to ask if we were lesbians because of the way you were so protective over me, trailing my decisions.

Mama's suggestion of us being flat mates was the greatest tie that bound us together and made people suspicious of us. I spoke to Mama last night. Despite Mama forbade me to, I wanted to tell you the outcome of our discussion.

Mama wanted someone to take her secrets to the grave, but she confided in the wrong person. I do not know how to keep my own demon to myself. But, I cannot break a mother's promise. I will obey her wish, which is why I am not narrating the story, the recorder is telling you, and therefore, I have not broken my promise.

As your birthday approaches, Mama had been on edge. Her blood pressure had increased ever since you insisted she must tell you and the pastor who your father is.

Gloria, Mama had no idea of your paternity. I know you are now holding the recorder, and your grip on it had tightened (she laughs insanely). You are not grinning I know, and what I am about to reveal is not funny; I am recounting this with great difficulty, you can now hear the tears in my voice.

Mama's father defiled her. On the same day, she ran away from home and sought shelter in an abandoned property; four men raped her. It was very dark when they took turns on her. Gloria, there was no way Mama could bring herself to tell you all these. You must wish you were not hearing this right now. Mama does not know which of the semen formed you.

Two years after your birth, she had an affair with Chief Daggers. Mama got pregnant with me. I am your blood sister. Gloria, our bond was not ordinary. Chief had told Mama to abort the pregnancy that it would be a taint to his reputation to have an illegitimate child. Mother had me without his knowledge, and put me in my parents' care, my foster parents. She followed my growth and saw I had good education.

She arranged for our paths to cross, Mama predestined everything. She never foresaw I would one day become Chief's lover. I have been having sex with my own father. I felt so dirty knowing this. I did not appreciate Mama telling me. Now you know why Mama took my fall.

After a long walk, I went to the police station and pleaded to the officers to let me have a talk with her, there I learned of the truth. I came back in the morning, I wanted to tell you, and for you to hold me, I needed your consolation, the news would shatter you, but I needed more consolations.

Gloria, I had been sleeping with my father. I am happy he is dead, I feel like killing him again. I came into your room to see you had torn our pictures. I knew then how much you despised me.

It really hurt me, Gloria. Therefore, by the time you might be listening to this, I would have left the city. I cannot be close to the city that will have my mother's blood on its surface, and a sister that hates me so much. (Rachel crying.)'

Her solemn goodbye awakened Gloria to the fact that she would lose all the family she had in the world. The tortuous journey of life had bent Gloria to the curviest of situation. She thought about combing the city before Rachel left for good.

Ezekiel slowly walked down the pedestrian lane. He scrolled through his small keypad phone to call the bus driver he was expecting from the capital city with a parcel. A mini bus wisp passed him and something nudged Ezekiel to look closely at the passenger seat.

Gloria was leaving town. After a final peace talk and sensitisation assignment in some rural communities, it was time to resume at the Naval Headquarters. After rigours of assignments and success, she was on the move to her new state of deployment. She would make new colleagues and lead a normal military life.

She tried not to think of the heartbreaks she nursed. She glanced at Rachel sleeping at the back seat. Gloria smiled at her tired sister. They had packed all night. She was leaving every memory and whatever emotional attachment she had with the town and the man who had stolen and released her heart.

Ezekiel and Gloria's eyes locked for a brief second. He waved her to halt but she just stared expressionlessly back at him. Ezekiel started running to catch up with the speeding vehicle, but he soon realized he was no Cheetah. He stopped and dialled Gloria's phone number after months, but the operators' tone said such subscriber did not exist on its network.

Gloria looked at her phone for his call, but remembered she had changed all her mobile numbers. He was the last person she expected to see in the city. She thought he had gone out of the city. He never looked for her because he thought lowly of her and her parentage.

Memories of their kisses flooded her mind. The one reason her sanity was still intact was that Ezekiel had prevented them from making love in the garden that night. It would have been hard for her to leave the colony had she known him beyond kisses and caresses.

www.ingramcontent.com/pod-product-compliance
Lightning Source LLC
Chambersburg PA
CBHW030601130626
46552CB00006B/2629